hhhhhhhhhhhhhhh . . .

My sweater is itchy,
my pants too tiiiight. . . .

NO MORE CLOTHES
FOR ME TONIGHT!

THE PROBLEM WITH PAJAMAS

Super un-comfy?

Times a *million.*

But you made it! Good work!

Thanks.

Now we can sit back and relax!

LAUREN STOHLER

ATHENEUM BOOKS FOR YOUNG READERS | New York London Toronto Sydney New Delhi

Sometimes I have un-comfy days!
I want to throw my clothes away!

Nothin' feels right,
and nothin' feels good,
even when everyone says that it should.

It's hard to explain,
so I wrote this song:
My clo-o-othes done me wrong!
Whoooaaaaaaaahhhhh.
Oh yeah,
my clo-o-othes done me wrooong.

Ahhh, well, here we are!
You and me! Pajama-free!
I don't miss my pajamas at all, do you?
Pajamas— HA! What are they even good for?
Staying warm?
Psh! We're perfectly toasty!
Feeling cuddly?
Bah! Who's cuddlier than we are?

CODY
Keeping tickly, prickly cat hairs off your shoulder? *Huh!* Who cares if they feel like itty-bitty spider feet?
Wait . . . what?
What? Don't cat hairs feel like itty-bitty spider feet to you?

I *love* pajamas.

rustle
rustle

Ta-daaa!

hop
hop

hop

To Gareth, who gets it

ATHENEUM BOOKS FOR YOUNG READERS · An imprint of Simon & Schuster Children's Publishing Division · 1230 Avenue of the Americas, New York, New York 10020 · © 2022 by Lauren Stohler · Book design by Karyn Lee © 2022 by Simon & Schuster, Inc. · All rights reserved, including the right of reproduction in whole or in part in any form. ATHENEUM BOOKS FOR YOUNG READERS is a registered trademark of Simon & Schuster, Inc. Atheneum logo is a trademark of Simon & Schuster, Inc. · For information about special discounts for bulk purchases, please contact Simon & Schuster Special Sales at 1-866-506-1949 or business@simonandschuster.com. · The Simon & Schuster Speakers Bureau can bring authors to your live event. For more information or to book an event, contact the Simon & Schuster Speakers Bureau at 1-866-248-3049 or visit our website at www.simonspeakers.com. · The text for this book was set in Allatuq. · The illustrations for this book were rendered digitally. · Manufactured in China · 1121 SCP · First Edition · 2 4 6 8 10 9 7 5 3 1 · Library of Congress Cataloging-in-Publication Data · Names: Stohler, Lauren, author, illustrator. · Title: The problem with pajamas / Lauren Stohler. · Description: First edition. | New York : Atheneum Books for Young Readers, [2022] | Audience: Ages 4-8. | Audience: Grades K-1. | Summary: After a long, itchy, uncomfortable day in clothes, a slew of fuzzy friends and her understanding Dad convince Cody that not all pajamas are bad. · Identifiers: LCCN 2021019381 | ISBN 9781534493438 (hardcover) | ISBN 9781534493445 (ebook) · Subjects: CYAC: Pajamas—Fiction. | Bedtime—Fiction. | Fathers and daughters—Fiction. | Toys—Fiction. · Classification: LCC PZ7.1.S7529 Pr 2022 | DDC [E]—dc23 · LC record available at https://lccn.loc.gov/2021019381